SpongeBob's Secret Valentine

By David Lewman
Illustrated by Heather Martinez

"Ready, Gary?" asked SpongeBob. His pet snail looked up and blinked. "Okay . . . fetch!" yelled SpongeBob as he lobbed a ball of kelp over Gary's head.

"Meow," said Gary, watching it fly by.

"Good effort, Gary!" said SpongeBob enthusiastically.

Sandy walked up with the kelp ball splattered all over her helmet. "Howdy, SpongeBob! Is this yours?"

"It sure is, Sandy!" he said. "Wanna play fetch with Gary and me?"

Sandy scraped the blob off her helmet and tossed it to him. "Sorry, SpongeBob, but I have to get home and make a special valentine for tomorrow. Adios!"

"Did you hear that, Gary?" asked SpongeBob. "I bet that special valentine Sandy's making is for me. I'd better start making one for her!"

"You like Sandy!" bellowed Patrick, who had crept up behind SpongeBob, startling him.

"Of course I like Sandy, Patrick. She's my friend."

"No, I mean you *really* like her," said Patrick. "If a boy gives a girl a valentine, it's a *really huge deal!*"

SpongeBob looked puzzled. "What do you mean?"

"Now you'll have to spend all your time with Sandy and you won't have time for any of your friends," explained Patrick. "Oh, SpongeBob, I'll miss you, little buddy!" With that, he ran off crying.

"Patrick, wait! Come back!" SpongeBob turned to Gary and shrugged. "You know, Gary, it's hard to believe, but I think Patrick might be wrong. On the other hand, I really don't want to lose any friends."

SpongeBob thought hard. Then he snapped his fingers. "I know! I'll ask Squidward!"

SpongeBob knocked on Squidward's door. "Squidward! Open up! It's an emergency!"

Squidward opened the door in a panic, dripping wet from his bath. "What? What's the emergency?" he asked, panting.

"Squidward, do you think I should give Sandy a valentine tomorrow?" Squidward just stared at SpongeBob. Then he slammed the door.

"Hmm, Squidward seems busy," said SpongeBob. "Maybe I'll ask Mr. Krabs."

At the Krusty Krab, Mr. Krabs leaned back in his chair. "Sure, SpongeBob, I'd be glad to give you some advice. Save every penny you make—"

SpongeBob interrupted him. "I don't need advice about money, Mr. Krabs. I need advice about a girl."

Mr. Krabs leaped up and yelled, "Stay away from me only daughter, SpongeBob!"

SpongeBob looked confused. "I'm not talking about Pearl, Mr. Krabs. I'm talking about Sandy."

"Oh," said Mr. Krabs, wiping his brow. "That's a relief. What seems to be the problem?"

SpongeBob explained the whole valentine situation.

"Hmm," replied Mr. Krabs, scratching his chin. "As she is a land creature, there's really no telling what Sandy will think of your valentine. I suggest you go over to her treedome."

SpongeBob brightened up. "To ask her?"

"No!" answered Mr. Krabs. "To *spy* on her."

SpongeBob disguised himself as a piece of coral and sneaked up to Sandy's treedome.

Then, very quietly, he pressed his face against the glass. He looked all around but didn't see Sandy anywhere. "Oh, tartar sauce!" said SpongeBob. "She must be inside her treehouse. I've got to go in."

SpongeBob opened and closed the door to the dome as quietly as he could and shimmied up the tree. He peeked through the window and saw Sandy making a huge, red valentine.

Suddenly, her nose twitched. "I smell saltwater," she said. "Either my dome's sprung a leak, or there's an . . . INTRUDER!"

SpongeBob scrambled down the side of the tree and out of the dome as fast as he could. He could hear Sandy behind him yelling, "You'll never get away, ya thievin' varmint!" But he did get away—just barely.

SpongeBob slammed the front door behind him and leaned up against it, breathing hard. "I've got to get to work," he told Gary. "Sandy's making me the biggest valentine I've ever seen! I don't care what Patrick says—I'm going to make one for her!"

SpongeBob dove into his closet and came out with his arms full of materials. Then he flew into action: drawing, cutting, and pasting until the sun came up over Bikini Bottom.

"I'M READY!" he shouted at last, holding up a big, beautiful valentine with Sandy's name on it.

SpongeBob ran over to Sandy's place with the valentine. Just as he reached her treedome, Sandy came out carrying her huge valentine.

"Hey, Sandy!" said SpongeBob, grinning. "That's quite a valentine you've got there. It must be for somebody pretty special."

Sandy nodded. "Yup, it sure is, SpongeBob. My mother's a very special lady!"

"M-m-mother?" said SpongeBob, stammering. "That's great, Sandy."
He tried to keep his big, fancy valentine hidden behind his back.
"Who's that valentine for, SpongeBob?" asked Sandy.
SpongeBob shifted his feet uneasily. "Um, what valentine?"
"The one that has 'Sandy' on it," she said.

Blushing, SpongeBob handed her the valentine. "It's for you, Sandy, but it doesn't really mean anything, like that I won't get to see Patrick anymore or . . ."

"Gosh, SpongeBob!" said Sandy, smiling. "This valentine's purtier than a Texas barbecue on the Fourth of July!"
Sandy held the valentine up, admiring it. Then she frowned. "You know what this means, SpongeBob?"

SpongeBob looked nervous. "No, Sandy," he said. "What does it mean?"
"It means I've got to thank you by challenging you to a karate match!"

Wow, thought SpongeBob, my friendship with Sandy hasn't changed a bit. Patrick was wrong!

"HEEEYAH!" yelled Sandy, flying through the air.

"HEEEYAH!" screamed SpongeBob.

And they spent the rest of Valentine's Day happily chopping away at each other.